THIS WALKER BOOK BELONGS TO:

_____

_____

_____

_____

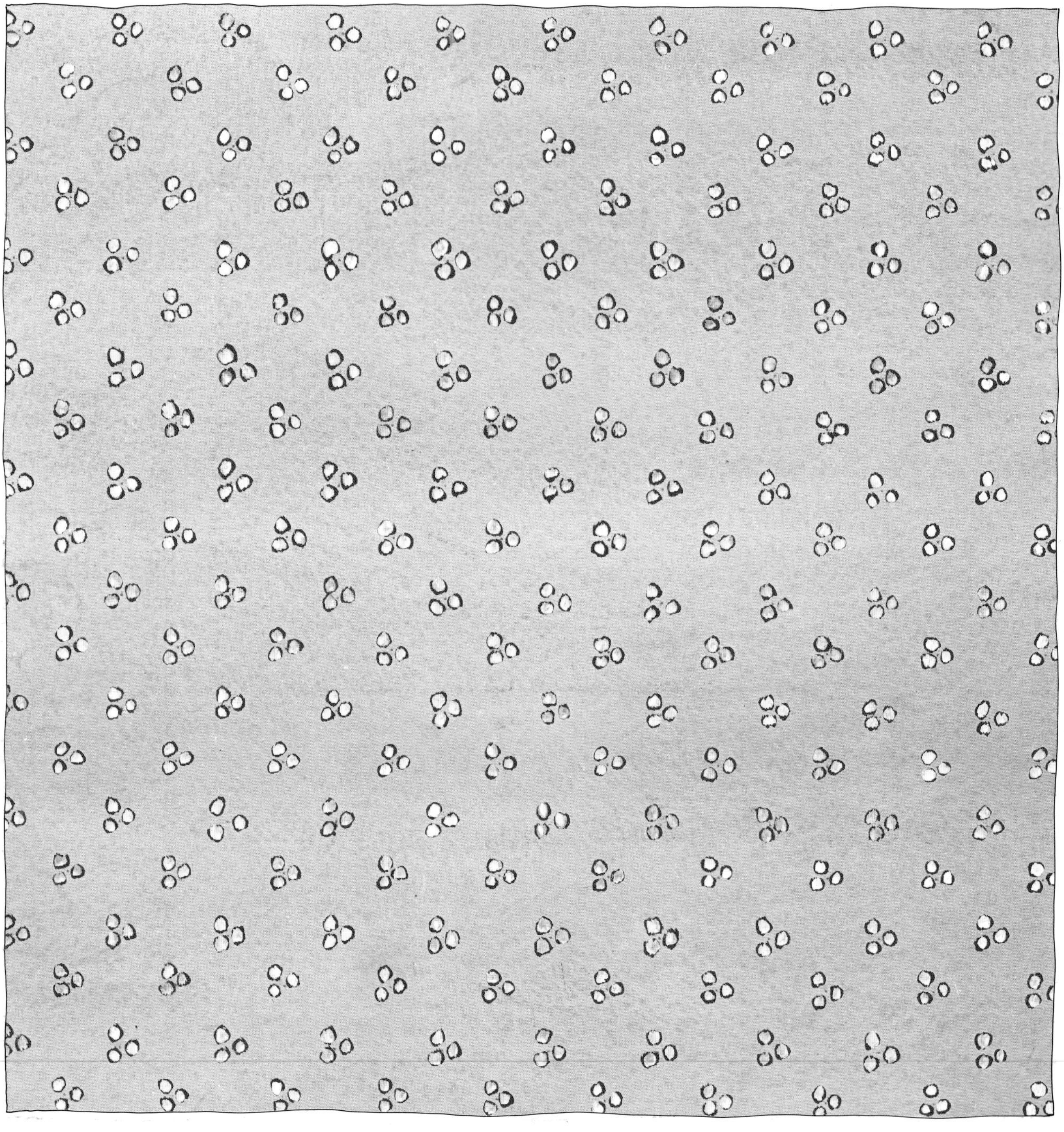

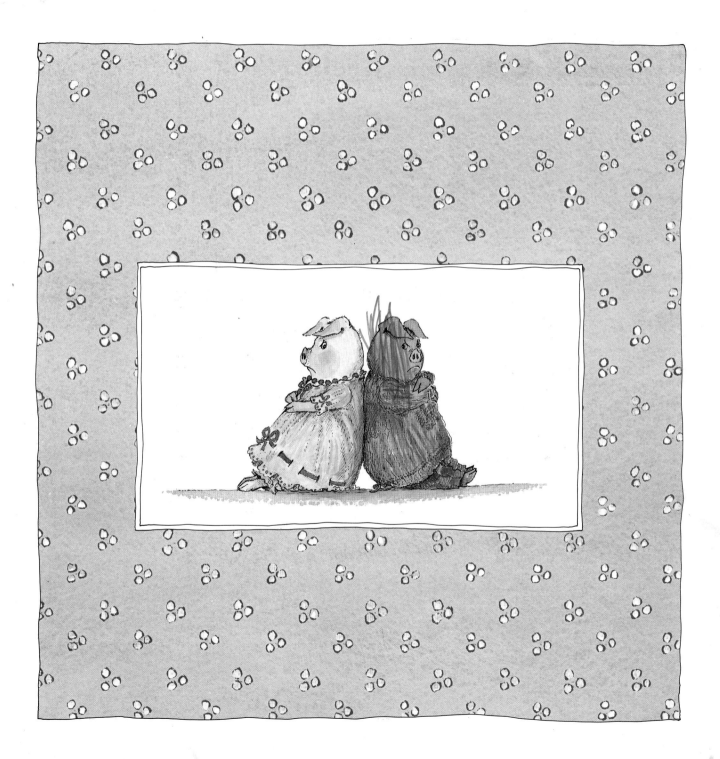

For
Emily, Sophie, Felix and Ben

First published 1985 by Walker Books Ltd
87 Vauxhall Walk, London SE11 5HJ

This edition published 2003

2 4 6 8 10 9 7 5 3 1

© 1985 Helen Craig Ltd

The right of Helen Craig to be identified as author/illustrator of this work has been
asserted by her in accordance with the Copyright, Designs and Patents Act 1988

This book has been typeset in M Baskerville

Printed in China

British Library Cataloguing in Publication Data:
a catalogue record for this book is available from the British Library

ISBN 0-7445-9457-X

The Night of the Paper Bag Monsters

HELEN CRAIG

WALKER BOOKS

AND SUBSIDIARIES

LONDON · BOSTON · SYDNEY

Susie was spending the day with Alfred.
He was worried. "We must think of something
to wear to the fancy-dress party tonight," he said.
"Shall we go as ghosts?" suggested Susie.

"Whooo, whooo, whooo!" howled the ghosts.
"Hello, Susie! Hello, Alfred!
 Having fun?" said Alfred's mother.

"This is no good," complained Alfred. "We must do
something so different that no one will recognize us."

In the garden shed they found
some very strong paper bags.

"Grrr, grrr, grrr!" growled Alfred. "I'm a terrible monster!"
"No, you're not," said Susie. "You're a pig in a
    brown paper bag!"

"Let's paint faces on the bags then," said Alfred,
   and they set to work.

Everything was going very well until Alfred stepped
back to admire his work. He accidentally knocked
a pot of green paint all over Susie's paper bag.

"Oh, you beast!" cried Susie. "You've ruined
all my work!" She picked up the tin of red paint
and poured it over Alfred's bag.

That did it. They started to quarrel and fight
and the paint went flying in all directions.

Susie sulked. "I want to go home," she said.
Alfred sulked and said, "I wish you'd never
come in the first place!"

"You're horrid!" exclaimed Susie, stalking off with
her half-finished, messed-up costume.
"Anyway," snorted Alfred, "I can do much better on my own!"

Back at her home Susie got out her sewing box and
the rag bag. "I'll show that Alfred," she muttered,
starting to snip and cut furiously.

Later in the day Alfred's mother brought something
to eat. "Where's Susie?" she asked.
"I don't know and I don't care!" Alfred replied.

Next door Susie's mother was surprised. "I thought
you were at Alfred's house," she said.
"I don't like Alfred any more," said Susie. "I'm
making my costume alone."

Night came and everything was quiet.
Susie's front door opened. A terrible monster appeared.

At the same time Alfred's front door opened.
Out stepped a second terrible monster.

The monsters met under the street lamp.

"HELP! HELP!" squeaked one of them.

"SOMEONE SAVE ME!" squealed the other.

"Ooh! Aah! EEEEK!" they shrieked wildly.

Suddenly they recognized each other's voices and
stopped and turned.
"Is that really you, Susie? You look fantastic!"
"And you look amazing, Alfred! Let's go
to the party together!"

So they set off.

On the way they were joined by all sorts of weird friends.

At the fancy-dress party they had games, lots of
lovely food and dancing. There was a competition
for the best costume.

Alfred and Susie won first prize together as Mr
and Mrs Monster. Their friend Sam came second.
Nobody knew the little person who came third.
He must have come from the other side of town.

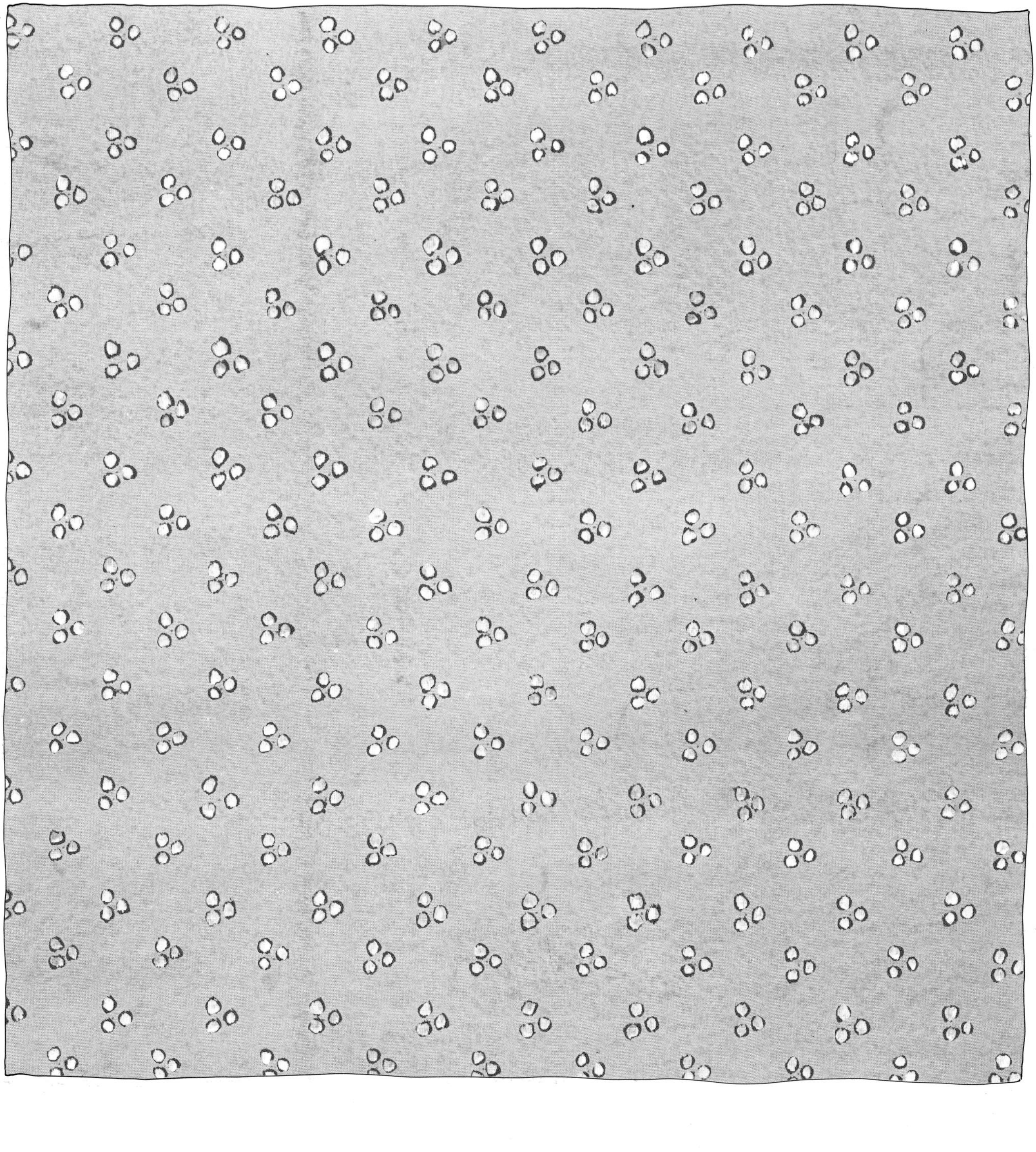